Look and Play

Racing Cars

by Jim Pipe

Aladdin/Watts

London • Sydney

racing car

2

Here is a
racing car.

3

fast

4

A racing car goes **fast**.

5

driver

6

Here is the **driver**.

start

8

This car is
at the **start**.

race

The **race** begins.

track

12

The cars race around a **track**.

fuel

This car stops for **fuel**.

15

tyres

This car needs new **tyres**.

17

finish

This car is first to **finish**.

18

19

What am I?

tyre

driver

engine

track

Match the words and pictures.

How many?

Can you count the racing cars?　21

Where am I?

22 Where are these cars racing?

Index

For Parents and Teachers

Questions you could ask:

p. 2 How many wheels does the car have? Four. Point out that the wheels are round. Ask the reader if they would work as well if they were shaped liked triangles or squares.

p. 4 Look at the spray! The wheels are making water spray up from the wet track. On rainy days the cars have special tyres to help them grip the track as water makes the track slippy.

p. 6 What is the driver wearing? He wears a tough driving suit and a crash helmet to protect his head. The place where a driver sits is the cockpit.

p. 9 What is the man doing here? He is wearing ear muffs to protect his ears from the noisy engines. Point out the grid that shows the car where to start.

p. 10 How many cars can you see? There are 20 or more cars in a race. At the start it can get very crowded and the cars can crash into each other.

p. 12 Do the cars drive in a straight line? No, the cars drive in a circle around the track. Each time they drive around it is called a lap. A race may last up to 60 or more laps.

p. 14 Why does the car need fuel? The engine needs fuel to make it go, like most cars. Compare with putting fuel into car at petrol pump, though in a race, the fuel is pumped in much faster.

p. 18 Can you describe the flag? A flag with black and white squares tells cars that they have finished.

Activities you could do:

• Encourage the reader to draw a racing car, writing labels for wheels, driver etc. Point out the flat shape of racing cars – this helps them go faster.

• Role play: ask reader to imagine they are driving in a race, e.g. getting in car, starting engine, steering the wheel, braking, crossing finish line.

• Show readers a tyre and other parts of a car, e.g. steering wheel, pedals, brakes, mirror. Look at the tyres and explain how the tread helps a car grip the road when it is wet and slippy.

© Aladdin Books Ltd 2008

Designed and produced by
Aladdin Books Ltd
PO Box 53987
London SW15 2SF

First published in 2008
by Franklin Watts
338 Euston Road
London NW1 3BH

Franklin Watts Australia
Level 17/207 Kent Street
Sydney, NSW 2000

All rights reserved
Printed in Malaysia

A catalogue record for this book is available from the British Library.

Dewey Classification: 629.228

ISBN 978 0 7496 8619 2

Franklin Watts is a division of Hachette Children's Books, an Hachette Livre UK company.
www.hachettelivre.co.uk

Series consultant
Zoe Stillwell is an Early Years teacher currently teaching at Pewley Down Infant School, Guildford.

Photocredits:
l-left, r-right, b-bottom, t-top, c-centre, m-middle.
All photos istockphoto.com except: 1 – Kiankhoon/Dreamstime.com. 2-3, 6-7, 14-15, 16-17, 20 tl, br & bl, 21, 23tl, blm, tr, tmr & br – Sergei Bachlakov /Dreamstime.com. 8-9, 10-11, 23bl – Ahmad Faizal Yahya/ Dreamstime.com. 23tr & bl – courtesy Mitsubishi Motors. 23br – US Army.